CAN A FOX WEAR POLKA-DOTTED SOCKS?
© copyright 1997 by ARO Publishing.
All rights reserved, including the right of reproduction in whole
or in part in any form. Designed and produced by ARO Publishing.
Printed in the U.S.A. P.O. Box 193 Provo, Utah 84603

ISBN 0-89868-302-5—Library Bound
ISBN 0-89868-303-3—Soft Bound

A PREDICTABLE WORD BOOK

CAN A FOX WEAR POLKA-DOTTED SOCKS?

Story by Janie Spaht Gill, Ph.D.
Illustrations by Bob Reese

ARO PUBLISHING

Can a fox wear
polka-dotted socks?

Can a bee watch t.v.?

Can a fly wear a tie?

9

Can a dragon ride in a wagon?

Can a goat drive a boat?

Can a rat swing a bat?

Can a bear shampoo his hair?

17

Can a cat wear a sunhat?

Can a mule go to school?

21

Can a fish
Make a birthday wish?

Can a bug give a hug?
I CAN!!